REFRIGERATOR Ball

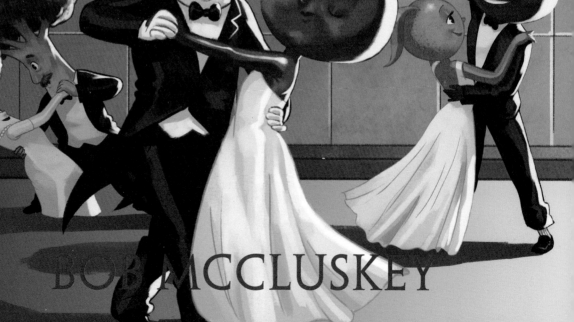

BOB MCCLUSKEY

REFRIGERATOR BALL
Copyright © 2016 by Bob McCluskey

ISBN: 978-1-4866-1340-3

Word Alive Press
131 Cordite Road, Winnipeg, MB R3W 1S1
www.wordalivepress.ca

WORD ALIVE
—PRESS—

Library and Archives Canada Cataloguing in Publication

McCluskey, Bob, 1926-, author
    Refrigerator ball / Bob McCluskey.

Issued in print and electronic formats.
ISBN 978-1-4866-1340-3 (paperback).--ISBN 978-1-4866-1341-0 (ebook)

    I. Title.

PS8625.C587R44 2016   jC813'.6   C2016-903615-4
                                      C2016-903616-2

This book is dedicated to every child whom
God created in His image: so perfectly.

Sometime through the night, when all were fast asleep,
something in the kitchen, started to stir and creak.
The refrigerator door opened, just a bit, and then
there was movement by the light that was lit.
The family pup was sleeping in the kitchen on the chair.
He woke up feeling foggy and began to stare at the
parade of fruits and veggies and began to growl.
The watermelon scared him, and he scooted with a howl!

Somehow they knew that nothing, would disturb their shiveree, 'cause the whole world was snoring, at half past three.

There was syncopated movement, as they stood on one spot, while the rubber band was tuning up, and stretching quite a lot.
When at last, in the rubber band, the elastics notes were true, they started playing nursery rhymes, that everybody knew.
All the fruit and veggies danced, oh how their feet flew, no worry about food groups, they were like a big stew!

So they paired off together, and it really was a sight, as they danced around the counter top, all through the night.
Mister Lettuce with Miss Tomato, and she blushed deep red, as twirling through the dancers, all around they sped.
For we know they blend together well, and well they should, 'cause a lettuce and tomato sandwich, tastes real good.

And different kinds of berries, were twirling in a bowl,
for blending all together, was tonight their goal.

I saw Mister Celery Stick, with his leafy top thatch,
waltzing Miss She's Whiz, they made a perfect match.

There goes Mister Broccoli, with prim Miss Cauliflower, looking lovely all in white, they danced by the hour.

Here they come, there they go, they put on quite a dancing show, 'round and 'round, in and out, gaily twirling all about.

Then the dawn was breaking... lights turned on up above, to dance another hour or two, they all would love.
Helter skelter they all rushed, down upon the floor, to the refrigerator fly, then opened up the door.
They jumped up to take their places, right where they belonged.
They had a lovely time tonight, and danced to every song.
They all were saying their goodbyes, they knew what did await, with all this hungry household, they'd soon be on a plate!
But don't be sad, they're really glad, they want to meet their fate, they know why God created them, and this makes them feel great!
So now into the kitchen, with sleep upon their face, come Mom and Dad for breakfast, finding everything in place.

They never dreamed what happened, as they glanced up at the clock, they'd really get an ear full, if that little dog could talk!

CPSIA information can be obtained
at www.ICGtesting.com
Printed in the USA
LVIC06n2226050517
533467LV00001B/1